Slothie
DIANA BORO
Illustrated by Zoe Reynolds

AuthorHouse™
1663 Liberty Drive
Bloomington, IN 47403
www.authorhouse.com
Phone: 833-262-8899

This book is printed on acid-free paper.

ISBN: 978-1-7283-7700-1 (sc)
ISBN: 978-1-7283-7701-8 (hc)
ISBN: 978-1-7283-7699-8 (e)

Library of Congress Control Number: 2023900546

Print information available on the last page.

Published by AuthorHouse 01/23/2023

authorHOUSE®

SLOTHIE

Written by: Diana Boro
Illustrated by: Zoe Reynolds

At the end of a quiet street, somewhat hidden by a blanket of lush, green trees, there lived a little girl and her stuffed animal, Slothie. They were the best of friends.

This little girl was named Star.

Star and Slothie were inseparable. Everything Star did, Slothie did too.

They ate breakfast together,

colored together,

watched movies together,

danced together,

and cuddled in bed together every single night.

Sometimes, Star would go on vacation, and can you guess where Slothie went?

That's right—Slothie came along too.

They learned new and exciting things every day. Star thought Slothie was all she really needed.

But there was still one dream Star had, and that was for her stuffed sloth to come to life. She wished Slothie would laugh with her like the kids at the playground did,

that Slothie would move on his own like the kids in Star's dance class,

and that Slothie would pick out outfits just like her mom did every day.

Star truly believed that it was possible. When she looked at Slothie, it was as if she saw magic that no one else could see.

One day, Star asked her parents whether they could travel to Costa Rica to visit the real sloths. She thought that if her Slothie was surrounded by other sloths, then something miraculous would happen.

Her family had traveled to many places, but they had never made it to Costa Rica to experience sloths up close and personal.

Her parents thought this idea was silly. "Stuffed animals can't come to life, sweetie," her mom said.

"Stop imagining things that are never going to happen," her dad said.

Even her little brother said, "No, no, sissy, it's not real."

But Star wouldn't take no for an answer.

She asked her parents every day, day and night, for one whole year. And every night, she would whisper to Slothie, "We're gonna make it; I know it."

On her seventh birthday, her parents surprised her with the biggest gift ever: round-trip plane tickets to Costa Rica. And even better, their flight left in one week.

Star was excited.

With one week till travel day, Star had so much time to learn about sloths. She checked out every book at the library and watched every documentary she could find. She knew she was ready.

And when travel day arrived, Star was the first one out the door to get to the taxi for a ride to the airport. She held Slothie tightly in a baby carrier, and away they went.

From the airplane window, Star and Slothie looked out over beautiful rainforest canopies. Everything looked so green and lush; it reminded her of her own home.

Costa Rica was everything she had dreamed of. It looked even better in real life. It was humid, warm, and tropical. The sun shone brightly, and she immediately felt Slothie warm up.

Star knew the magic was working.

On the third day of their travels, Star and her family went to visit a sloth sanctuary.

There, sloths who were injured or orphaned or who simply needed a place to live could do so safely. They had the right kind of people working with them to provide a better quality of life. Star learned so much.

She got the chance to hold a real sloth. And Slothie was next to her every step of the way.

Star knew the magic was working.

The next morning, Star went for a walk with Slothie outside the hotel grounds. She talked to Slothie about how it felt to be among real sloths. She shared her joy and her love.

And then, out of nowhere, Slothie replied, "It feels good to be home."

In that very moment, Star felt a sudden flash of magic overcome her. It was as if the whole world froze and she and Slothie became one.

Slothie asked Star, "Can we go visit my family today?"

"Of course! I would do anything for you," said Star.

The moment they reached the sanctuary, Slothie slowly made his way to the other sloths in the trees.

Star knew that real sloths spent almost their entire lives upside down. She knew they moved incredibly slowly.

She knew they could sleep very well all day long.

Star thought about her hopes and realized that maybe Slothie was better here, living with his own kind—having a good sloth life in Costa Rica.

Slothie would never be as fast as the kids at the playground, and he certainly would never be able to dance on two feet like the kids at her dance school.

And that was OK.

Star loved Slothie so much that she knew in her heart that his happiness would mean more to her than anything else. The fact that her stuffed sloth came to life was all the magic Star needed. Star also recalled that she could visit Slothie every time she came to Costa Rica.

On her final day of travels, she whispered to Slothie, "We made it, buddy. I told you we would."

Slothie replied, "Thank you for believing in me. With your love, we made our dreams come true. I am happy. I am home. And that's the true purpose of life, my girl—to be happy and to feel at home."

And at the end of a quiet street, somewhat hidden by a blanket of lush green trees, there lived a little girl named Star and her stuffed animal, Switch.

She had many stories to tell and many adventures that were to come. Star had all the magic she needed. She felt more alive and excited than ever.

She was happy, and she was home.

About the Author

Diana Boro is a children's book writer based in the Pacific Northwest. She received a BA in sociology and education from Principia College in Elsah, Illinois. She has been involved in many outreach programs and child advocacy efforts. In 2009 and 2010, Diana earned the Donald T. Bliss community service award in recognition of her love and time spent in the community. She also has a passion for everything African and dreams of one day opening her own orphanage or school in Kenya. *Slothie* is her first published book and was entirely inspired by her daughter. In her spare time, Diana enjoys trying new vegan recipes, taking photographs, learning Swahili, and going to the beach. Diana lives in the Seattle area with her husband, David, and their two children, Nova and Lovie King.

About the Artist

Zoe Reynolds is a Washington-based illustrator. She was born in Seattle WA and learned how to paint from her mom. She has been a part-time illustrator since 2018 and will continue to illustrate and publish children's books. Zoe's art carries a theme of the beauty of nature, fairytales, and history. Her focus throughout her books and illustrations is based on both mental and physical diversities to promote both inclusion and awareness. When Zoe isn't painting she is either dancing or studying to be a Marine Biologist at the University of Washington. You can see more of her art on Instagram @pinkquoi

Authors Note

Nova Nyakio Boro with her stuffed sloth, Slothie (2017)

Slothie on one of his many travels (Nairobi, Kenya 2020)

In 2017, my sweet daughter, Nova, got her stuffed sloth at the Woodland Park Zoo in Seattle, Washington. Little did we know, her stuffed sloth, Slothie, would become one of her dearest and most treasured friends. Nova and Slothie have traveled to many far away places, including: the Oregon coast, in our backpacks at Disneyland, across the border and up into Canada, over seas to Germany, Ethiopia and Kenya, just to name a few. My daughter was the inspiration and drive behind writing this book. I wanted her special bond with her stuffed sloth to be cherished forever and what better way than to dedicate and write a book completely for her.

Slothie is not your typical children's book. It is not predictable. It may end somewhat open ended. Some may be left wondering why the little girl left her sloth in Costa Rica. However, this was my intent in writing this book. I wanted the reader to determine for themselves the purpose of the story. To me, this book touches on a few different things. Firstly, that finding *happiness* and *home* are truly the greatest treasures in life. Secondly, the fact that the little girl was able to let go of her sloth was a lesson in sharing with others. Sometimes in life we do have to physically let go of things and most usually when we do, it is a blessing to someone else. In the case of my story, Slothie blessed a whole family of sloths in Costa Rica. Lastly, I used magic in this story to show the possibility of something unbelievable, happening.

It was the girl's faith in her sloth and love in her heart that helped the magic come to life. I also loved how the girl knew that her sloth was genuinely and completely happy living among other sloths in Costa Rica. This happiness was felt between them both. Their friendship would never die because true friendship remains strong even all the way across the world. And as you know, distance makes the heart grow fonder.

I hope this book can bring a smile to your face. I hope you can find a new love for sloths if you haven't already. Above all else, I hope you have also found your sense of happiness and home, wherever it may be.

To connect with the author:

Visit Diana on Instagram: @sproutedwithlove or Email: mamanyakio1515@gmail.com

10% of our book proceeds from Slothie will go to Sloth Sanctuary Costa Rica. You can find them online at www.slothsanctuary.com

CPSIA information can be obtained
at www.ICGtesting.com
Printed in the USA
LVHW072317170223
739816LV00006B/79